5-Minute
Fancy NANCY Stories

Based on the creation of
Jane O'Connor and Robin Preiss Glasser

HARPER FESTIVAL
An Imprint of HarperCollins Publishers

HarperFestival is an imprint of HarperCollins Publishers.

Fancy Nancy: 5-Minute Fancy Nancy Stories
Text copyright © 2015 by Jane O'Connor
Illustrations copyright © 2015 by Robin Preiss Glasser

ISBN 978-0-06-241216-4

Typography by Lori S. Malkin
16 17 18 19   SCP   10 9 8 7 6 5 4 3
❖
First edition

Contents

Fancy Words in this Book

Ami—friend (you say it like this: ah-mee)

Ancestors—people in your family who
    lived long ago

Appetite—hungry

Arrive—getting someplace

Au revoir—good-bye (you say it like this:
    aw ruh-VWA)

Belle—beautiful (you say it like this: bell)

Bonjour—hello (you say it like this: bohn-joor)

Brainstorm—a great idea

Canceled—called off

Celebrities—movie stars

Comfort—make someone feel better

Complicated—the opposite of easy

Concealed—hidden

Confess—tell about something
    bad you did

Curtsy—a bow

Deceased—dead

Demonstrate—show

Describe—tell about

Detest—hate

Dilemma—a problem

Diorama—a 3D display

Disgrace yourself—look like a fool

Dread—not looking forward to something

Ecstatic—happy

Elegant—fancy

Exaggerate—stretch the truth

Excluded—left out

Excruciating—to hurt very much

Exhausted—very, very tired

Exotic—out of the ordinary; from somewhere
    far away

Fascinating—extremely interesting

Faux pas—mistake (you say it like this: foh pah)

Flattering—pretty

Flawless—doing something perfectly

Fondly—with love

Frolic—jumping around and having fun

Ginormous—very, very big

Glamorous attire—clothes

Glorious—wonderful

Gore—blood

Gorgeous—beautiful

Huge—even bigger than big

Illustrate—make a picture

Imaginative—full of good ideas

Immature—babyish

Impress—wanting people to go "Wow"

In transit—on the way

Injure—hurt

Jovial—friendly

Joyful—happy

Lavatory—bathroom

Long for—really, really want

Making progress—getting better

Merci—thank you (you say it like this: mer-SEE)

Moment—a second

Odd—strange

Ordinary—plain

Outfit—clothes

Outing—short trip

Paparazzi—people who take
    pictures of models and celebrities

Perplexed—mixed up

Ponder—to think and think

Prefer—like one thing more than another

Prevent—stop something

Remind—make us remember something

Reply—answer

Revolting—yucky and gross

Slim—thin

Sob—noisy weeping

Spectacular—great

Speechless—too surprised to say a word

Splendiferous—excellent

Tardy—late

Terrified—scared

Transparent—see-through

Très magnifique—very cool or wonderful
    (you say it like this: tray ma-nifeek)

Unique—one of a kind

Unison—all together

Unkind—mean

Veranda—porch

Verse—a poem that rhymes

Voilà—look at this! (you say it like this: vwa-la)

Weeping—crying

Wise—smart and understanding

Fancy NANCY and the Late, Late, LATE Night

I adore visiting my neighbor Mrs. DeVine. Here we are having tea and sweets on her veranda. (That's a fancy word for porch.) I have my own special teacup at her house. It is shaped like a tulip. Mrs. DeVine says it reminds her of me—sweet and fancy. Of course, Jewel joins us too.

When she was a child, Mrs. DeVine lived in Hollywood. She used to see lots of movie stars. Mrs. DeVine calls them celebrities. Isn't that fancy?

Mrs. DeVine has movie posters covering her walls. "I was on the set of some of those films," she tells me. (A set is a place where they make movies.) She also has a special scrapbook of photographs. Some are autographed. That means celebrities signed them.

6

"Your scrapbook is extremely fascinating," I say.
(Fascinating is even more interesting than interesting.)

Ooh la la! Mrs. DeVine says I can borrow her scrapbook
if I bring it back tomorrow.

"*Merci, merci, merci!*" I say.

At home I pretend that I am a Hollywood celebrity. I dress up in my most glamorous attire—that's fancy for clothes. I put on my star gown, my turquoise heels, and my fuchsia and scarlet boa. I wear my sunglasses too. All celebrities do!

All my fans flock to see me. Lucky for them, I am feeling jovial. (That is fancy for friendly.) I sign so many autographs that my hand hurts.

Next, I pose for photographs with Frenchy. (Celebrities always pose with their dogs.) I am guessing that Frenchy and I will be in all the magazines tomorrow.

"I am late for a glamorous Hollywood party," I tell my fans.

"Au revoir!" (You say it like this: aw ruh-VWA. That's French for good-bye.)

On my door I put up a sign that says Do Not Disturb. Celebrities need their privacy. I want to look through Mrs. DeVine's scrapbook, but I hear my dad calling us all to dinner.

After dinner I learn all my spelling words. I am practically an expert at spelling, but it's always good to practice.

Ball B-A-L-L

Family F-A-M-I-L-Y

Thing T-H-I-N-G

Because B-E-C-A-U-S-E

Surprise S-U-R-P-R-I-S-E

Feather F-E-A-T-H-E-R

Before I know it, Mom says, "Nancy, time for bed."

Oh no! I haven't had a second to look at the scrapbook. I beg my mom to let me stay up later. But my mom says no.

"It's a school night," she says. "Tomorrow is Friday. Tomorrow you can stay up later."

I go upstairs and get
ready for bed. I brush my
teeth and put on my nightie.
My parents kiss me
good night.
"Sleep tight," they say.
"Sweet dreams."

But guess what! I am not going to sleep. Under the covers, I have concealed—that's fancy for hidden—a flashlight and Mrs. DeVine's scrapbook.

Frenchy, Marabelle, and I stay up very late admiring all of the celebrities. There are pictures at parties and movie premieres. How glamorous! It's almost ten o'clock when I put away the scrapbook and turn off my flashlight. I bet even celebrities don't stay up this late!

The next morning, when my
dad wakes me up, I am exhausted.
Exhausted is even worse than tired.
I can hardly get out of bed.

At recess, I am too exhausted to jump rope with Bree and my friends. They play double Dutch—one of my favorites. But I can barely even stand up and watch them.

My brain is exhausted too. When it's time for the spelling test, I miss three of the words on the list.

After school, I return Mrs. DeVine's scrapbook. I tell her that Frenchy, Marabelle, and I stayed up most of the night poring over all of the fabulous photos. I thank her for letting me borrow it.

She asks if I would like to stay for dinner and watch a movie called *National Velvet*.

"It's on TV tonight. It is a wonderful story about a girl
and a horse," she says. "I loved it when I was your age."

It sounds fascinating, but I can hardly keep my eyes
open. I promise to stay for dinner and a movie another time.

I go home and start weeping—which is fancy for crying. When my dad asks what's wrong, I confess.

"I was naughty," I say. "I stayed up late last night looking at Mrs. DeVine's scrapbook. I had a terrible and exhausting day! I even got three words wrong on my spelling test!"

My dad doesn't scold me. He says, "Now you understand why you need a good night's sleep."

That night I go to bed even earlier than my sister. I can hardly stay awake for the bedtime story Dad reads to us. (Neither can Frenchy.)

On Saturday I wake up feeling glorious again. (Glorious is fancy for wonderful.) And guess what—Mrs. DeVine taped the movie for me! I can see it tonight.

Dad was right—even fancy girls need their beauty rest.

Fancy NANCY Hair Dos and Hair Don'ts

"Do not forget. Tomorrow is Picture Day," Ms. Glass reminds us. (Reminding is fancy for making us remember something.) "I also have a surprise."

"Ooh! Ooh!" says Clara. "I love surprises. What is it?"

"If I told you, it wouldn't be a surprise," says Ms. Glass. "You will find out tomorrow."

"Good-bye," I say to Ms. Glass.

"See you tomorrow, Nancy," says Ms. Glass.

Ms. Glass didn't need to remind me about Picture Day. It is just about the most important day of the school year. Weeks ago I put a circle around the day on my calendar.

Weeks ago I practiced my best smile. Weeks ago I picked out my outfit. (Outfit is fancy for clothes.) I will wear my pink shirt with ruffles, my purple skirt with ruffles, and my pink-and-purple socks with ruffles. Ruffles make anything fancy!

After dinner, I read my library book. It is about Amelia Earhart. She was a brave airplane pilot. She was the first woman to fly solo across the Atlantic Ocean. That means she flew all by herself. One day, as she was flying, her plane disappeared. No one knows what happened to her. It is a mystery.

Amelia was not fancy. But I like how she
looks, her hair most of all. Her hairstyle is called
a bob. Then it hits me. I have not decided on my
hairstyle for Picture Day!

My hair is curly, so I can wear it in many flattering ways. (Flattering is fancy for pretty.) Maybe I will wear my hair in pigtails. Maybe I will wear my hair in a bun. Maybe I will wear my hair long and loose.

Just then Bree calls. She describes her outfit for Picture Day. (Describe means to tell about.) "I am going to wear my green shirt and my green layered skirt," she says.

"I am also going to wear my brown boots with the butterflies."

"Ooh la la," I say. "You will look marvelous!"

Then she says, "My mom braided my hair and put in new colored beads."

"Oh, how elegant," I tell her. (Elegant is fancy for fancy.)

Maybe I will wear cornrows like Bree. But Mom is busy. She does not have time to make lots of braids. And Dad is not a good braider. He tries, but he just doesn't have the right technique. (That means he hasn't really learned how to do it yet.)

"It's okay," I tell him. "I will figure something out."

Later I read more of my book about Amelia Earhart. I learn that Amelia used to have long hair, but she cut it short. Then it hits me. I will wear my hair like Amelia.

Ooh la la! That will be perfect for Picture Day. Amelia's hair was shorter than mine. But that is not a problem. Not a problem at all! I can trim my hair.

I snip a little here. I snip a little there. I snip in the back. And I snip in the front for bangs. Snip, snip, snip!

I look in the mirror. My bangs are crooked. So I snip just a little more. Trimming hair is very complicated! (Complicated is the opposite of easy.) Now I understand why the stylists (these are the people who cut hair) have to go to a special school.

I am still snipping when Mom comes into my room. "Nancy!" she says. "What are you doing? Scissors are only for cutting paper. That is a Clancy family rule."

"I'm sorry," I say. "Really I am. I just wanted my hair to look perfect for Picture Day."

But now that I look at my hair . . . it looks horrible!

Mom tries her best to help. She snips here. She snips there. She evens out my bangs.

"There," she says. "Your hair looks fine."

She is trying to comfort me. (That's fancy for making me feel better.) But I don't really feel better. My hair looks dreadful (that's worse than bad).

I will ruin the whole class picture.

"I can't go to school tomorrow," I say. "I can't be in the picture."

But Mom says, "You are not missing school because of your hair."

The next morning,
I come into class. I am
wearing my fancy outfit. I have
tied a scarf around my head. It does
not look fancy. It looks odd—which is
fancy for strange. Luckily, no one really
seems to notice.

Soon it is time for the picture. Lionel and Bree are next to me. I wish I could hide. I wish I were invisible. I wish this day would just end!

Ms. Glass says, "You all look wonderful. Now I will show you the surprise." She has caps for us. The caps say "Ms. Glass's Stars."

"Do you want to wear the caps for the picture?" Ms. Glass asks.

"Yes!" we shout.
(I shout louder than
anybody.)

Quickly I unwrap my
scarf. I put on my cap. I
do not look odd anymore.
I look almost normal!

One, two, three. We all
say, "Cheese!"
   And for the moment—
that's fancy for right now—
I look picture-perfect!

Fancy NANCY and the Too-Loose Tooth

It is recess. Lionel and I are swinging on the monkey bars. Lionel swings upside down.

"Whoo! Whoo! I am an ape!" Lionel shouts, and scratches under his arms.

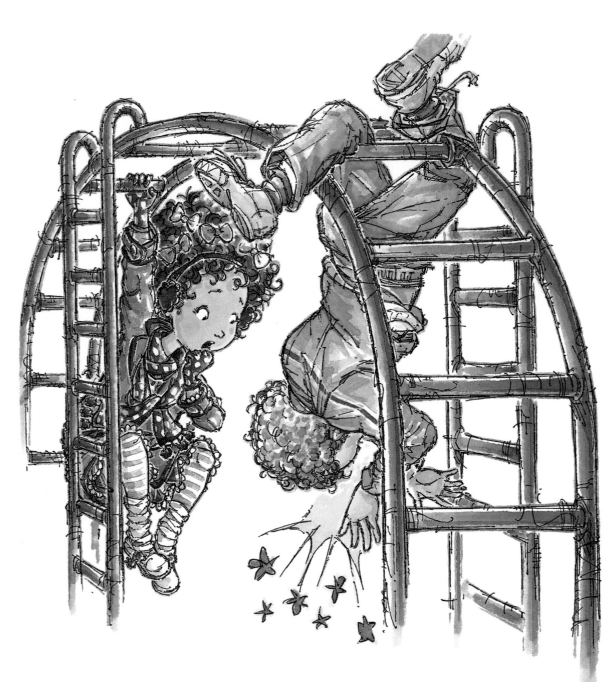

Lionel swings again. He bangs into a bar.

"Ow!" he says. "That hurt!"

Lionel jumps to the ground. I jump down too. His hand is over his mouth. There is a little gore! (Gore is a fancy word for blood.)

"Come quick, Ms. Glass!" I shout.
"Lionel banged into the monkey bars.
He is injured." (That's fancy for hurt.)
Ms. Glass rushes over to Lionel.

"I am okay." Lionel
smiles.
That's when I
notice! He lost a
tooth! It is in his hand.
"It was already
loose," he says.

Ms. Glass lets me go to the nurse with Lionel. First Lionel washes out his mouth. Next he washes his tooth. Then the nurse hands Lionel a white plastic tooth on a chain. *Pop!* The top opens. In goes the tooth. *Pop!* The top snaps shut.

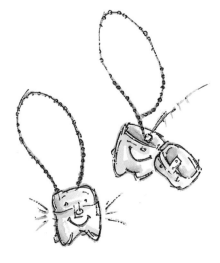

It is *très magnifique!* That is French for very, very cool.

For the rest of the day Lionel wears
his tooth necklace. I long for a tooth
necklace too. (That
means I really,
really want one.)
But you only get
one if your tooth
falls out at school.

I excuse myself to go to the restroom. I need to check my teeth. I wiggle each one. Guess what? One of my teeth is loose now. Not super loose—just kind of loose. It better not fall out at home!

"It absolutely must fall out at school," I say to myself in the mirror. "Then I can get a tooth necklace just like Lionel's."

All week my tooth gets looser and looser.
I wiggle it a lot at school. I wiggle it at recess.
I wiggle it in art class. I wiggle it at lunch.

At home I do not wiggle my tooth at all. I eat a lot of soft stuff, like bananas and ice cream. That way, it is less likely to fall out.

I don't talk much either. Talking might make my tooth fall out.

My dad asks, "Want me to pull out your tooth? It won't hurt."

"No!" I shout.

It can't fall out at home!

On Thursday at school, my tooth is hanging by a thread. I keep waiting for it to fall out. I wiggle it and wiggle it. I wiggle it with my finger. I wiggle it with my tongue. The day goes on and on, but my tooth does not fall out. I can't believe it. I thought for sure that it would have come out by now. When the last bell rings, my tooth is still stuck in my head.

Now I am very worried that my tooth will fall out at home. I must prevent it from falling out tonight. (Prevent means to stop something.)

I put a little tape around it. There! That should do it.

It does look a little funny, though.

"What's wrong with your mouth?" my mom asks.

I do not dare talk. It cannot fall out now. I write a note to explain.

My tooth is very loose.

I don't want it to fall out until I'm at school.

Then I'll get a tooth necklace, like Lionel's.

That night, I sleep with my mouth open.

I am not taking any chances.

The next morning, I check my tooth.
The tape worked! My tooth is still hanging
there—just barely. I get dressed very carefully.
I start walking to school when all of a sudden
something tickles my nose.

"Achoo!" I sneeze.

Oh no! Sneezing made my tooth fall out. It's in my mouth! I am not at school yet. So does this mean I don't deserve a tooth necklace? But my tooth is still in my mouth. So, in a way, it has not fallen out yet. I keep my lips shut tight. I walk very fast. At last I arrive at school. (Arrive is fancy for getting someplace.)

I find Ms. Glass. I spit my tooth into my hand.

"I just lost a tooth!" I shout.

Ms. Glass sends me to the nurse. I wash out my mouth. I wash my tooth.

Ooh la la! The nurse gives me a tooth necklace.

My tooth necklace looks so fancy. I wear
it all day. But guess what? I do not feel joyful.
(That's fancy for happy.)

Finally I confess. Confess means telling about something bad you did. I tell Ms. Glass that my tooth did not fall out at school. Not really. I tell her how I was walking to school and I sneezed—and that is when my tooth fell out.

"I think I need to return the tooth necklace," I say.

Ms. Glass thinks for a moment. (A moment is fancy for a second.)

"Your tooth didn't fall out at home," she says. "You were already in transit. That means on the way to school. I think that counts."

But just to be sure, Ms. Glass checks with the nurse. The nurse agrees. The tooth necklace is mine to keep forever!

For the first time all day, I smile a big smile—with a hole in it!

Fancy NANCY and the Mean Girl

This Friday is Field Day. There will be races and a picnic at school. Almost everyone is excited. But one person is dreading it. (That's fancy for hoping Field Day never comes.)

That person is me.

Ms. Glass hands out our T-shirts. I am not on a team with my friends. But that is not why I dread Field Day. I get a green T-shirt. I prefer the red T-shirt. (Prefer means I like it more than mine.) But that is not why I dread Field Day.

Here is the reason. I am not a good runner, and I am in the relay race. Last year my team lost because of me. I tried to run fast, but I was very slow.

Everyone raced past me. I got teased.

At recess Grace is wearing her T-shirt. It is green. Oh no! We're on the same team! Grace can be unkind sometimes. (That's fancy for mean.)

"I am in the relay race," Grace says. "It's a good event for me because I am fast. Are you in the relay race, Nancy?" she asks me.

I wish I could tell her no. I wish I could tell her that there is a new event this year and that I am doing that. But I cannot. I nod. "Yes, I am in the relay race," I say.

All Grace says is "Rats, now we'll never win!"

At home I turn on the TV. I want to see the weather report. Maybe it will rain. Then Field Day will be canceled. (That's fancy for called off.)

But it's going to be sunny and hot. Rats!

I worry and worry about Field Day. But then I have a marvelous idea. Maybe if I practice a lot, I can get faster by Friday.

Every afternoon I run
and run. Frenchy keeps me company.
She doesn't run with me. She just watches.
But that's okay. I am glad she is here. She is like
my own private cheerleader. I run every day. My
legs burn, but I keep running. I time myself to see
if I am getting any faster. But I am not. It is no
use. I was born with slow legs.

On Thursday at recess
I hear Grace say, "I'm stuck
in the relay race with Nancy.
She is so slow! My baby
brother runs faster than her."
Isn't that unkind?

At lunch I have no appetite. (That means I'm not
hungry.) I don't even finish my cupcake. Field Day is
tomorrow. I am going to disgrace myself! (That means I'll
look like a fool.) I wish there was no such thing as Field Day.

Lionel is so lucky. He broke his leg two weeks ago. His doctor said that he can't be in any races. His doctor sent a note to school saying that he had to take it easy, even at recess.

Then I get a splendid idea.

On the way home from
school, I pretend to trip.
"Ow! Ow!" I say. "I think I
injured my foot." (Injured is fancy
for hurt.) I limp home.

I limp into the dining room. I bring a piece of notepaper and my lucky pen. My sister helps me to the table. I tell my parents, "I don't think it's wise for me to run in the relay race tomorrow. I might hurt my foot worse. You'd better write a note and tell Ms. Glass that I can't run because my foot is injured."

Later my dad comes into my room. He inspects my feet. (That means that he looks them over very carefully.)

"Nancy, is your foot really hurt?" he asks.

"How can you ask me that?" I say.

My own father doesn't believe me!

So my dad says, "Well, sometimes you limp on your right foot. And sometimes you limp on your left foot."

All of a sudden I start sobbing. Sobbing is like weeping, only much more noisy. I am a bad runner, but I am a worse fibber!

I tell my dad about the relay race and what Grace said at recess. He listens. He nods. He really understands!

We talk for a long time. I feel much better.

On Field Day I am not limping. I wear
my green team T-shirt. I wear lace-trimmed
socks for good luck. I cheer for my team. (I
am splendid at cheering.)

Soon it is time for the relay race. I go up to Grace. I do not use any fancy words. "I will run as fast as I can," I say, "but if we lose, don't say mean stuff. You are a good runner. But you are not a good sport."

Grace sits down at the picnic table. She is speechless! That means she is so surprised she can't say a word.

The relay race starts. Grace is very fast. She runs all the way to the cone and then starts back. She is way ahead of the other runners.

Grace taps me.

Now I start to run to the cone. I have a big head start. I go as fast as I can. But soon the other runners go past me. I come in last—just like last year. We lose the race. I feel so bad.

At the picnic, Grace comes over. Uh-oh! But guess what? All she says is, "Want a cookie? My mom baked them."

So I say, *"Merci,"* and take one.

And guess what?

My appetite is back.

Fancy NANCY
Sand Castles and Sand Palaces

Ooh la la! We are going on a summer outing—that's fancy for a short trip. It takes us a long time to pack. We want to make sure we have everything we need. Bree is coming with us.

Look! Here she is now.

Can you guess where we are headed? If you think it's the beach, you are 100 percent correct! Bree and I help my mom pack the car. At first, my mom is not sure if everything will fit, but somehow we stuff it all in.

Frenchy sits in the front seat. She loves going to the beach! She likes to chase the seagulls and dig in the sand.

Do you see the lovely sunbonnet I made for her? I think she likes it!

The car ride takes forever. The traffic is terrible, awful, and horrendous! Cars are honking. People do not look happy.

"It's okay," my mom says. "It's just part of going to the beach."

I wonder if we will ever get there. It seems like we are hardly moving. Bree and JoJo get sleepy. But not me. I am too excited to sleep. I decide to make Frenchy look like a glamorous beach movie star!

Ooh la la, Frenchy! You look magnificent!

Now we have to stop at a gas station because JoJo needs to use the lavatory. (That's fancy for bathroom.) Mom gets the key from the lady at the front. Soon we are back on the road.

Finally we arrive! The beach is very busy. We have a hard time finding a parking spot. Can you see where our car is parked? I will give you a hint. It is parked between a green car and a purple car.

We find a great spot to put up the umbrella. Bree and I put our sunbonnets by the blanket so they don't get wet. Then we run down to the ocean to frolic in the waves. Frolic is fancy for jumping around and having fun. We toss the beach ball back and forth. Frenchy tries to get the ball, but we keep it away from her because we don't want it to pop.

Soon it is time for refreshments. Bree and I drink fizzy fruit juice from a can. Then we have Popsicles. Bree picks lime. I pick strawberry cream. JoJo makes a big mess with her grape Popsicle. Luckily, Frenchy is here to help clean her up!

Mom says that everything tastes better at the beach. I wonder why? Maybe it's because of the salty air.

Now we get down to serious business—building the fanciest sand castle ever. First, we build up a ginormous (that's fancy for very, very big) pile of sand. Then we get some buckets of water. They are very heavy! Next we shape the sand using sand pails and water. Everybody helps.

My mom shows us how to decorate the towers. You hold the sand in your fist and let it dribble out from the bottom.

Voilà! It looks gorgeous!

While my mom reads, Bree, JoJo, and I go around the beach collecting shells in our buckets. We find a bunch of different kinds. We even find some sand dollars! We use the shells to decorate the walls.

"Check it out!" Bree says and giggles. "My shell is crawling away!"

JoJo wants to float her boat, so Bree and I dig a moat all the way around the castle. I step back to admire our work.

"Ooh la la," I say. "This isn't a sand castle. It's a sand palace!"

"I think it's the best one we've ever made," says Bree.

She is correct. Our sand palace is spectacular.

After so much hard work, we all agree that more
frolicking in the waves is what we need.

"Come on," says Bree. "Let's play mermaids!"

Bree and I play mermaids for a long time. We even
make up a silly dance where we have to bump tummies.
JoJo and her sea horse watch. They really like it!

Bree and I want to put on a big show for JoJo—a fancy seaside show—but my mom says that the waves are getting too big. It is too dangerous to stay in. We have to come out.

That is when we see our sand palace.
"Oh no!" Bree says. "Look what the waves did."
"Our sand palace is in ruins!" I say.

JoJo starts crying, but I am more mature. That's because I have been to the beach many times before.

"The beach never runs out of sand or shells," I tell my sister. "We can build an even bigger and better sand palace."

So that is exactly what we do. And this one is even fancier than the last! It has a winding staircase, more floors, and a flag at the very top.

What a marvelous day at the beach!

Fancy NANCY
Budding Ballerina

I absolutely love ballet! My friend Bree and I go to Madame Lucille's Academie of the Dance. Madame Lucille was once a prima ballerina. (That means she was one of the best ballerinas ever.) Bree and I have class every week. Madame Lucille shows us how to be graceful and have good form. She is a tough teacher and makes us work hard, but that makes us better ballerinas.

We do not dance on our toes yet. But one day we will. That is called *en pointe*. (You say it like this: ahn pwant.)

Today my dad and Frenchy pick me up after class. I demonstrate (that's fancy for show) what I learned today.

"Dad, watch this," I say. "It is an *arabesque*." (You say it like this: ara BESK.) I stand on one leg. I hold my other leg straight behind me, and I point my toes.

"It takes a lot of balance. It is hard to do it with good form. Do you see how my toes are pointed? Madame Lucille says that we must always point our toes," I tell him. "Practice makes perfect."

I tell Dad all about the things we learned in class today.
Dad holds the door open for me as I *pirouette*—that's like
twirling—into the house. Frenchy wags her tail. That's her
way of telling me how graceful I am.

"*Merci*, Frenchy!" I say.

88

"Dad, you *pirouette* now," I suggest.

"Right now? Right here?" he asks.

"Sure!" I say. "It's fun! Try it."

Dad spins. He tries his best, but he loses his balance. Oops!

"I guess that I'm not a natural dancer like you are," he says.

"Dad, you must have a positive attitude," I tell him. That means he has to believe in himself.

"*Pirouettes* are hard. You should start with something easier. Don't worry. I can help you," I say.

Ooh la la! Suddenly I have a stupendous idea.

"I'll be right back," I tell him. "Don't go anywhere."

I dash up to my bedroom. I find my glitter pens and a big piece of paper. I make a sign. Then I bring it downstairs.

When Dad sees the sign, he is ecstatic. That's fancy for happy.

"Your class starts in ten minutes," I tell him. "You better change out of your work clothes and into something more flexible."

Dad is very prompt. He shows up right on time.

"Welcome to Nancy's Dance Academy," I say. "I am so glad you came. Let's get started right away."

"Oh, I forgot my tutu!" Dad says.

I giggle. He is just being silly. Only girls wear tutus!

"We will begin with the five basic ballet positions," I say. "Here is first position. Not to brag, but my technique is flawless." (That's fancy for doing it perfectly.)

Dad is working on first position when the door opens. It's Mom and JoJo back from the store.

"Welcome to Nancy's Dance Academy," I say. "You can join the beginner class too. The more the merrier."

I show the class how to do second, third, and fourth positions. They are all doing pretty well, but by the time we get to fifth position, Dad's legs are all tangled up.

Dad trips and falls over. JoJo and Mom giggle. Frenchy runs over to make sure he is not hurt.

"It's okay, Dad," I say. "You are making progress." (That's fancy for getting better.) "Ballet takes a lot of practice!"

93

We are just about to begin again when the doorbell rings. I tell my students that they may take a break. They sit down on the couch to rest their legs. I answer the door.

It's Bree! What perfect timing! Now I have another stupendous idea. . . .

"You have all worked hard, especially Dad. Now we will perform for you," I tell the class. "Bree and I have been in ballet class for over a year now. Watch and learn."

Bree and I *plié* (You say it like this: plee-ay) . . .

we *jeté* (You say it like this: je-tay) . . .

and we do many
pirouettes.

At the end, we curtsy—a fancy way of taking a bow.
"Bravo!" everyone cheers.

Bree and I are happy with our progress. Our hard work
shows. Madame Lucille would be proud of us.

97

Later I get out my glitter pens again. I make a giant award for Dad.

"Here," I tell him. "Thank you for coming to Nancy's Dance Academy today. You earned this. You worked very hard. You're the real budding ballerina."

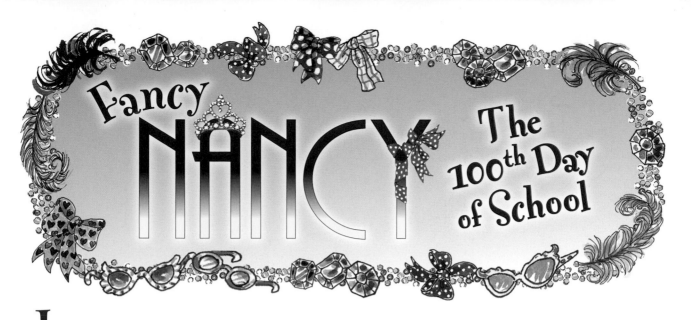

Fancy NANCY
The 100th Day of School

It is the 97th day of school, and I have a dilemma. (That is a BIG problem.) I do not know what to bring in for the 100th day.

All my friends have ideas. Bree put 100 feathers on a hat. It looks so elegant! (That's a fancy word for pretty.)

Robert is bringing his stamp album. There are 100 stamps in it. The stamps are from countries all over the world.

At school, Yoko shows me her piggy bank.
It has 100 pennies. The bank is transparent.
(That means you can see inside.)

Lionel made a ball out of 100 rubber bands.
"I have been saving them for about five years," he tells me.
I wish I had something to show my friends.

After school, I look all around my room. I dig in my drawers. I dump everything out on my bed. I have 39 hair clips. That is not enough.

I have 57 bracelets. That is not enough. I have 84 ribbons. That is not enough.

What am I going to do?

Now it is the 98th day of school. More kids bring in stuff. Teddy brings in a bag with 100 marbles. Macy brings in a jar with 100 jelly beans.

JP brings in a box with 100 crayons. It seems like everyone has an idea. Everyone but me.

I tell Ms. Glass my dilemma. She tells me not to worry.

"You are very imaginative," she says. "That means you are full of good ideas. You will think of something."

That makes me feel a bit better, but I still wonder: Will I be able to find something by *Friday*?

At home, I tell Mom my dilemma.

"Everybody has brought their one hundred things in already," I tell her. "Everyone but me."

Mom is making dinner. She dumps macaroni into a pot of boiling water.

"I know," she says, "how about a poster with macaroni?"

I do not want to hurt Mom's feelings, but three kids have already done stuff with macaroni. Macaroni is not imaginative. I do not want to do anything with macaroni.

I go downstairs. Dad is doing the wash. Maybe he will have a good idea. Dad says, "I bet we have fifty pairs of socks. Fifty times two, that makes one hundred."

I do not want to hurt Dad's feelings. But socks are ugly. I can't bring them to school!

I want something imaginative and fancy.

After dinner, I try to think some more. All of a sudden, I hear my sister crying. I rush into her room.

"What's wrong, JoJo?" I ask.

"Look," my sister says.

JoJo points at her fishbowl. Goldy is her goldfish. Goldy is not moving.

Goldy is floating on top of the water.

We bury Goldy in our backyard. We all come to pay
our condolences (that means that we all tell JoJo how sad
we are for her that her fish died). Everyone is sad, even
Frenchy. I am so glad that dogs live a long time.

We put a few pebbles from Goldy's bowl on top. I tell
my sister, "We will remember Goldy fondly." Fondly means
with love.

The next day, I write a poem. It is about Goldy. Ms. Glass likes my poem. She reads it to the class.

Goldy was gold.
For a fish, she was old.
She liked to swim,
So she stayed slim.
You can't kiss a fish.
But you can miss a fish.

"Nancy uses interesting words," Ms. Glass says. "Slim means thin. Her poem is in verse. It rhymes."

Ms. Glass's kind words make me so happy that I almost forget that tomorrow is the 100th day of school. But I don't forget and then I start to worry. What am I going to do?

At home, it is sad to see the empty fishbowl. Mom is about to throw out the pebbles. Then, all of a sudden, I get an idea that is imaginative.

"Stop!" I say. "Don't throw the pebbles away. I need them!"

I wash and dry all the pebbles.
They are so pretty.
I count them.
Yes! There are 104!

I get my markers. I get a huge piece of paper. Huge is even bigger than big. I will make a poster.

I spell out Goldy's name in glitter. I draw a picture of Goldy in her bowl. Then I glue on the pebbles. I let my sister help.

There are 100 pebbles

I write on the poster, "There are 100 pebbles in the fishbowl."

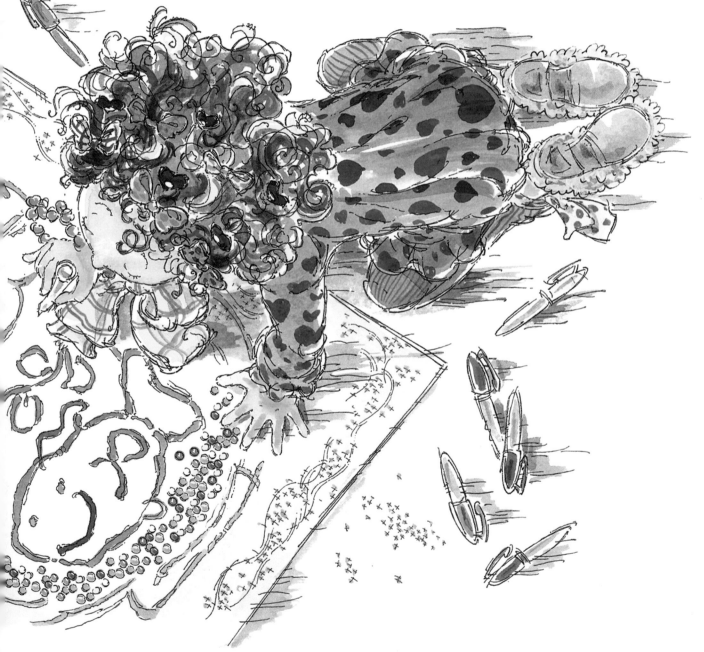

Today is the 100th day of school. I bring in
my poster. I made it just in time! Ms. Glass brings
in something too. It's a cart with 100 books.

She will read them all to us before school
ends in June. Ms. Glass is so imaginative.

Fancy NANCY Pajama Day

"Class, don't forget!" Ms. Glass says, pointing to the calendar. "Tomorrow is . . ."

"Pajama Day!" we shout in unison. (That's a fancy word for all together.)

"You may all bring in one stuffed animal," Ms. Glass says. "And a blanket for story time."

We all cheer. We love Pajama Day!

I plan to wear my new nightgown. I just got it last week when my grandma was visiting. We went to the big department store downtown.

The nightgown is white and lacy. Grandma even bought a matching one for Marabelle. I must say, they are very elegant! (Elegant is a fancy word for fancy.)

A little later, the phone rings. It is Bree. She says, "I am going to wear my pajamas with pink hearts and polka dots. Do you want to wear yours? We can be twins!"

"Ooh!" I say. "Being twins would be fun."

Then I look at my elegant nightgown. What a dilemma!

(That's a fancy word for problem.)

All night I think about what I should do. Should I wear my new elegant nightgown or should I be twins with Bree? It is such a hard decision!

Finally I make up my mind. I call Bree.

I tell her that I am going to wear my brand-new elegant nightgown.

"The one my grandma bought for me," I say.

"Okay," she says.

I can tell Bree is disappointed, but I know she understands.

Bree is my best friend. She knows how much I love being fancy.

The next morning at school, we can't stop laughing. Everyone's in pajamas, even the principal. He is wearing blue-and-white-striped flannel pajamas, and he is carrying a teddy bear. His teddy bear is wearing striped flannel pajamas too!

Ms. Glass has on a long pink nightshirt with red polka dots. She is wearing fuzzy red slippers.

"That looks warm and cozy," I tell her.

I glance around the room. I am the only one in a fancy nightgown.

That makes me unique! (You say it like this: you-NEEK.)

"Let me look at you," says Ms. Glass kindly. "What a beautiful nightgown!"

"*Merci,*" I say.

"Nancy, look!" says Bree, waving. "Clara has on the same pajamas as me."

I look and see that Bree is right. Clara and Bree are both wearing pajamas with pink hearts and polka dots—just like the ones I have at home.

Bree and Clara giggle.

"We're twins!" says Clara.

"And we didn't even plan it," says Bree.

At story hour, Ms. Glass has us spread out our blankets. She reads us a bedtime story. It is about a genie and a magic lamp. There is even an exotic princess in it. It is a good story, but it is difficult for me to concentrate. That means I am having a hard time listening.

Clara and Bree lie next to each other. "We're twins," Clara keeps saying.

At recess Clara takes Bree's hand. They run across the playground to the monkey bars. They hang upside down and laugh. Bree smiles and waves to me.

"Come on, Nancy," she calls. "Come join us!"

But it is hard to climb in a long elegant nightgown. And I certainly can't hang upside down. Everyone would see my underpants!

At lunch I sit with Bree and Clara. They both have grape rolls in their lunch boxes. I wish my mom had packed me a grape roll.

"Isn't that funny, Nancy?" asks Clara. "Bree and I even have the same dessert."

I do not reply. (That's a fancy word for answer.) Pajama Day is not turning out to be much fun. I wanted to be fancy and unique. Instead I feel excluded. (That's fancy for left out.)

I am sad to say
that the afternoon is
no better. Clara and
Bree are partners in
folk dancing. They
twist and twirl. They
swing and step.

They have a
great time.

My partner is Robert.
He trips and steps on my
hem. Some of the lace on
my nightgown rips. One of my
flower hair clips pops out of
my hair.

"I am really sorry, Nancy,"
he says.

I can tell he feels
bad about it.

"It's okay," I tell him.
But I don't feel very okay.

At last the bell rings. I am glad Pajama
Day is over. I pack up my bag and go find Bree.
"Do you want to come play at my house?"
I ask her. "We can do whatever you want."

But Bree can't come. She's going to Clara's house! I know it's immature. (That's fancy for babyish.) But I almost start to cry. Then, as we are leaving, Bree and Clara rush over.

"Nancy, can you come play too?" Clara asks.

All of a sudden the day seems brighter.

"Yes!" I say. "I just have to go home first to change."
I rush home and find my pajamas with pink hearts and polka dots.

Now we are triplets!
Clara, Bree, and I spend the rest of the
day making three of everything.

Fancy NANCY
My Family History

Do you know about your ancestors? They are people in your family who lived long ago. (You say it like this: ANN-sess-terz.)

Isn't that a great fancy word?

We are writing ancestor reports in class. Bree is writing about her great-grandfather. He is ninety. He was a war hero. He saved a whole bunch of soldiers from dying. He even earned two medals. Bree is going to bring the medals to class.

Robert's great-grandmother is one hundred. She came to America on a steamship when she was a little girl. While she

was on board, she got the chicken
pox. She had to be quarantined. (You say
it like this: kwawr-uhn-teend.) That means she had to be put
in a separate cabin so that other people wouldn't get sick.

"You are both lucky," I tell my friends. "You know your
ancestors. All of mine are deceased." (That's fancy for dead.)

That night my grandpa calls. He is coming to visit soon. His parents are my great-grandparents. So I ask, "Were they famous? Did they have adventures?"

Grandpa laughs and says no. "They were nice ordinary people."

Ordinary? That's like plain. I wish I had fancy ancestors.

I wish my ancestors were kings and queens. Or maybe movie stars.

Later that night, Grandpa sends a photo of my great-grandfather.

Grandpa's email says, "My dad was a kind and honest man. He only lost his temper once. I broke my mother's favorite teapot and blamed my little sister. My dad wasn't upset about my mother's teapot. He was upset that I lied to him."

"Your dad sounds like a very lovely person," I reply. (Reply is fancy for answer.) "I am going to write my school report about him."

I gather all kinds of facts from Grandpa. My ancestor had five children. He was a guard for a bank in New Jersey. He liked to go on vacation and fish. He wore glasses and liked to golf. He lived to be seventy-four.

The next day I illustrate the cover. (Illustrate is fancy for making a picture.) Then I start writing my report. It begins, "My great-grandpa was a bank guard."

Hmmm. That does not sound exciting. In fact, it sounds very dull.

137

So I add something extra. "Once he stopped a bunch of bank robbers. They were notorious (that means famous in a bad way) criminals, so the mayor gave him a special medal at a banquet." A banquet is a fancy dinner honoring someone.

Yes! That sounds very exciting.

Next I write, "My great-grandpa loved to fish." Then I add some more exciting stuff. "One time while he was in Fiji, he caught a giant shark!"

The next day Clara and Yoko both read their reports. Clara tells about her great-grandma who lives in Mexico. Yoko tells about her great-grandfather. He is a chef. She brings in a bumpy vegetable that he grew in his garden. I do not mean to brag, but my report is way, way, way more interesting.

After school, I tell my parents, "On Friday I get to read my ancestor report!"

My dad says, "Great! Grandpa is coming on Thursday. He can go to school with you. He is so proud that your ancestor report is about his dad."

I forgot about Grandpa coming. All of a sudden, my tummy feels funny. "I don't think he is allowed to come," I say.

My mom looks at me. "Of course he can come," she says. "Don't you want him to?"

I don't know what to say, so I run upstairs to my room.

When Mom comes upstairs, I show her my report. "I wanted it to be interesting," I say, "so I exaggerated a little bit." (Exaggerate is a fancy word for stretching the truth.)

"Honey," Mom says, "you didn't just exaggerate a little bit. You made stuff up. That's lying."

Lying? I remember the story about the broken teapot. My ancestor would not like that I made stuff up about him. My grandpa will not like it either.

By the time Grandpa comes, I have written a new report. This time I stick to the plain truth. I write that he had five kids. I write that he was a bank guard. I also write about my grandpa breaking the teapot. It is an ordinary story. But I really like it.

On Friday Grandpa comes to school.
He has brought his dad's top hat. It's
a real one, not like the one from
the magic set I got for my birthday
last year.

"My great-grandpa loved to
get dressed up," I tell everyone.
"I must get being fancy from
him!"

Fancy NANCY Spring Fashion Fling

Ooh la la! Spring is in the air. All of the flowers are in bloom. They are so fragrant (that is fancy for smelling good).

Bree, JoJo, and I are going to decorate Easter eggs. First we hard-boil the eggs. Then we spread newspaper out all over the table. Finally we get to the fun part—painting colorful designs on them!

"Look at this one!" I say, holding up my favorite.

"It's beautiful," says Bree. "Do you like mine?"

I tell her I think it's fantastic. "I especially like the pink tulip on the bottom part," I say.

We say nice things about JoJo's eggs too.

After we finish decorating all of the eggs, I say,
"What else can we do that would be extra special
for spring?"

We ponder—which means we think and think and
think. Finally I have an idea.

"What about a fashion show for our dolls?" I say.

"Yes!" Bree says. "That's a great idea! We can call
it Spring Fashion Fling. We can invite our parents."

"And Mrs. DeVine," I say. "She loves fashion!"

We line up all our models. Marabelle and Chiffon and
Sarinda. We must create the perfect ensembles for them to
wear. We want to impress the crowd—that means we want
them to go "Wow!" The outfits have to look like nothing
anyone's ever seen before.

Bree and I pore over the glamorous fashion magazines. We pin up our favorite designs. Then we use the pinups for inspiration as we draw our own designs. We have big, big plans for our Spring Fashion Fling.

As we are drawing our own designs, Bree has a brainstorm! That's a fancy way of saying she has a great idea.

"Wouldn't it be great if we could use real flowers in our designs?" she says.

What a splendiferous idea! (That's fancy for excellent.)

Mom agrees. She helps us cut some flowers from her garden.

JoJo makes a headpiece for Sarinda with a white-and-lavender flower. Bree drapes Chiffon with a garland of daisies. I add some pink and blue carnations to Marabelle's gown.

We make sure each ensemble is unique. That means it's one of a kind.

"Perhaps we will be fashion designers when we grow up," Bree says.

"We could work in Paris, France!" I say. "Wouldn't that be glamorous?"

We have some leftover flowers so we use them on our invitations. They turn out beautiful!

We deliver our invitations personally. The invitations tell everyone what time to come and that brunch will be served after the show.

151

Bree and I are feeling a little frazzled. We are exhausted. It is a lot of work putting together a fashion show! But the invitations are delivered and Mom has even set a beautiful table. The show is going to be extraordinary!

Spring Fashion Fling!

V.I.P.

V.I.P.

We have one final touch before the fashion show. We set up the runway—that is where the models walk to show the designs.

Bree thinks that the models look a little nervous.

"They will be fine," I tell her. "They probably just have a few pre-show jitters."

Ooh la la! It is finally time for the Spring Fashion Fling. We show everyone where to sit.

"I saved this seat for you," I tell Mrs. DeVine. "You will be the first to see the models come down the runway."

Mrs. DeVine gives me a squeeze. "I can't wait," she says. "I am sure it will be marvelous!"

Dad and Freddy are the paparazzi. (They're the people who take pictures of models and celebrities.) They start taking pictures even before the show starts.

155

I am about to start the show when
something tragic happens. I trip! I grab
the tablecloth to get my balance, but I
accidentally pull too hard.

What a fashion faux pas! (That means a mistake.)
Is everything ruined?

157

No! The show goes on! The paparazzi help me
to my feet. The audience quickly cleans up the mess
just as the next models come down the runway.

It's JoJo and Frenchy! They are superb (that means really, really good). They walk down the runway (without tripping) and show off our lovely fashion designs.

At the end, we get a standing ovation. Everyone stands up and claps like crazy.

Then we sit down to brunch. All that work has made us very hungry. We eat fancy sandwiches, fruit, and salad.

During brunch, I make a toast. "To JoJo and Frenchy, the stars of the fashion show!"

Everyone cheers. I already can't wait to start working on my summer collection!

Fancy NANCY and the Boy from Paris

I almost always get to school early. But on Monday I am tardy. (That's a fancy word for late.) I come in and see a new kid. He has black hair and is wearing a red-striped shirt. He is standing next to Ms. Glass.

"Robert comes from Paris!" Ms. Glass is telling everyone. "He just moved here last week."

Paris! Paris is a city in France. It is gorgeous. (That is a fancy word for beautiful.)

"Let's give him a big welcome!" says Ms. Glass.

Everyone in the class claps. I clap the loudest of all.

161

Later that day, I see Robert in the book nook.

"*Bonjour,*" I say. (In French that means hello.) "I am Nancy. I've never met anybody from Paris before. I am pleased to make your acquaintance." (That means that I am happy to meet him.)

I speak slowly so he will understand.

"It's really nice there," Robert says. "I miss it." He has a book on cowboys. I guess he probably wants to learn all about this country. That's what I would do if I were in a new country.

"I want to go there someday." I show him my book.
It is about a dog named Fifi that lives in Paris. Fifi has
many adventures. In the last story, Fifi got trapped in
the Eiffel Tower.

"Do you like the United States?" I ask him.

"Yes, I do," says Robert. "Don't you?"

"Yes, I like it very much," I say. "I've lived here all my life."

Then Ms. Glass puts a finger to her mouth.

"This is not talking time," she says. "This is reading time."

On Tuesday I sit next to Robert at lunch. "Have you ever been to the Eiffel Tower?" I ask him.

Robert nods and swallows. "Lots of times. Our house was near it. I could see part of it from the playground at school."

I tell Robert, "I know about the Eiffel Tower. There's a poster of it in my room. I know lots about Paris."

I share some of my lunch.
"These are donut holes," I say.
Robert gives me a funny look.
"I know that," he says. "I have eaten donut holes before."

That night while my mom and dad are making dinner, I tell them about Robert. "He is very nice," I say. "He already speaks English. He is trying to learn all he can about our country. He is mostly interested in cowboys. I want to be his friend. How do you say friend in French?"

"The word is *ami*," my mom says. "You say it like this: ah-mee."

I love French. Everything sounds so fancy!

"Why don't you ask him over to play?" my dad says.

What a great idea!

So the next day I do.

"We can play soccer," I say. "Did you play soccer in Paris?"

"Sure. All the time," Robert says. "I was on a soccer team. I am a good kicker. I can come on Friday."

On Thursday it is Show and Share. Robert brings in a plastic toy horse. It is brown and white. "My grandpa has a horse like this," he says.

He looks a little sad.

Robert passes around a photo. "I miss her a lot. I gave her carrots every day. Sometimes I even got to ride her. Her name is Belle. In French that means beautiful."

"*Belle,*" I say to myself. Now I know another French word.

On Friday Mom is at work. Mrs. DeVine picks us up from school. "Mrs. DeVine lives next door," I tell Robert.

"Robert is from Paris," I tell Mrs. DeVine. "Isn't that wonderful?"

Mrs. DeVine smiles. "Paris is a lovely place," she says.

Robert is quiet. I think he misses Paris a lot.

At home we make a tent in the yard. We pretend bears are outside. We pretend to be terrified. (That's a fancy word for scared.)

Then we put on our cleats and play soccer. We let my little sister play too. Robert is a great kicker. He kicks the ball really far!

My dog runs around the yard. She loves to chase balls.

"That's Frenchy," I tell Robert. "She is not really French. But you will like her anyway."

We go inside and I show Robert my room. "See?" I say, pointing to the poster on my wall. "There's the Eiffel Tower."

"But that one does not have a cowboy hat on it," Robert says. "That Eiffel Tower is in Paris, France. It is taller, and it is more famous. But we have an Eiffel Tower too. Our Eiffel Tower has a cowboy hat on the top."

Wait a minute. I am very perplexed. (That's a fancy word for mixed up.)

"But you're from Paris, France," I say. "Aren't you?"

"No, I am from Texas. Paris, Texas," Robert says. "Ms. Glass told everybody that the first day."

Robert shows me Paris, Texas, on my globe.

Oh! I guess I missed that part. And I feel a little silly. But not for long. After all, I have a new *ami*, even if he isn't French.

Fancy NANCY

Peanut Butter and Jellyfish

Ooh la la! Our class is on a field trip. We are at the aquarium. We will see all kinds of amazing creatures that live in the sea.

First we have lunch in the aquarium cafeteria.
"Look," says Ms. Glass. "The chairs look like waves."
After I find a wave chair, I open my lunch box. Inside
is a peanut butter and jelly sandwich, celery sticks
with peanut butter, and peanut butter cookies. I
should not be surprised.

"The other day, my dad made peanut butter,"
I tell Clara and Bree. "He made way too
much. Now everything he prepares
for me has peanut butter!
Pretty soon I am going to
turn into a peanut."

Soon it is time to see the exhibits. We see tropical fish in every color you can imagine. The tank is so big, it seems like we are inside the ocean.

We watch sea otters playing. We see a dolphin show. There is even a pool with manta rays that we can touch. (They feel like wet sandpaper!) We have to put our hands in the water slowly so that we don't scare them.

Then we come to a special exhibit. The sign in front says The Wonders of Jellyfish. "I don't want to go in," I say. "I detest jellyfish." (Detest is a fancy word for hate.)

Once, at the ocean, I got stung by a jellyfish. It was excruciating—that is fancy for hurting very much.

"Don't look at them," Bree tells me. "Just shut your eyes and hold on to me. I will tell you when it is over."

"*Merci, mon ami*," I say. (That's French for thank you, my friend.)

I close my eyes as Bree leads me through the jellyfish exhibit. Oops! I bump into someone. Oops! I bump into someone else.

"Pardon me," I say.

Then I hear someone say, "Nancy, is something the matter?"

I open my eyes partway. It is Ms. Glass. I explain why I detest jellyfish. Ms. Glass says, "I understand. I once got stung by a jellyfish. It does hurt! But they are amazing sea creatures. Come look."

Ms. Glass takes one hand. I cup my other hand over my eyes so I only have to look a little.

We pass by a glass case of big, blobby, brown jellyfish.
"Ew! Revolting!" I say. (That means yucky and gross.)
But Ms. Glass keeps insisting that jellyfish are amazing.
"Jellyfish don't have eyes or ears," Ms. Glass says.
"They don't have bones or a heart. They are made mostly
of water. The long strings are tentacles. Those are what
sting. Often jellyfish sting to defend themselves against
an enemy."

"I was not an enemy!" I tell her. "I was just swimming
and having fun."

"Yes, but the jellyfish had no way of knowing that,"
Ms. Glass says. "Jellyfish don't have brains, either."

I guess I see what Ms. Glass means. The jellyfish wasn't out to get me. It's not smart enough to do that. I just happened to be swimming where the jellyfish was.

Ms. Glass stops in front of a case of purple jellyfish. They aren't nearly as revolting as the brown jellyfish.

Next we stand in front of a case where there are lots of blue jellyfish.

"Look, Ms. Glass," I say. "They are transparent." (That means you can see right through them.)

Ms. Glass smiles at me. "Pretty amazing, don't you agree?"

I nod as we walk to another case.

These jellyfish look like pearly pink bubbles.

In the very last case are tons of tiny jellyfish with lights. They blink on and off like fireflies. I am not so scared anymore. I have decided that Ms. Glass is right. Jellyfish are amazing!

That night, I tell my family about the aquarium and about all of the different kinds of jellyfish I saw.

"I am going to make a jellyfish diorama for Ms. Glass," I say, "because she helped me overcome my fear."

I explain to JoJo that a diorama is a 3D display.

I get to work right after dinner. I find an empty shoe box and paint the inside blue. Then I stick long, pink ribbons onto one of Mom's old shower caps.

Ooh la la! It looks just like a jellyfish!

Dad helps me hang my jellyfish from the top of the shoe box. Then he clears the table. (No one ate much dinner. It was chicken with peanut butter sauce.)

"Too bad I don't have sand for the bottom," I say.

"Hold on," Dad tells me. "Wait one minute."

Dad goes into the kitchen and comes back with the giant jar of homemade peanut butter. We spoon the last of the peanut butter onto the bottom of the shoe box until the jar is empty.

"It looks exactly like sand," I say.

Well, maybe not exactly, but it's good enough. I stick seashells into the peanut butter sand.

Voilà! It looks spectacular. (That's fancy for great.)

The next morning, I present the shoe box to Ms. Glass. "Oh! A jellyfish diorama!" she exclaims.

Then I giggle and say, "No, Ms. Glass. It's a peanut butter and jellyfish diorama!"